Brian Wildsmith
Whose shoes?

Oxford University Press

Oxford Toronto Melbourne

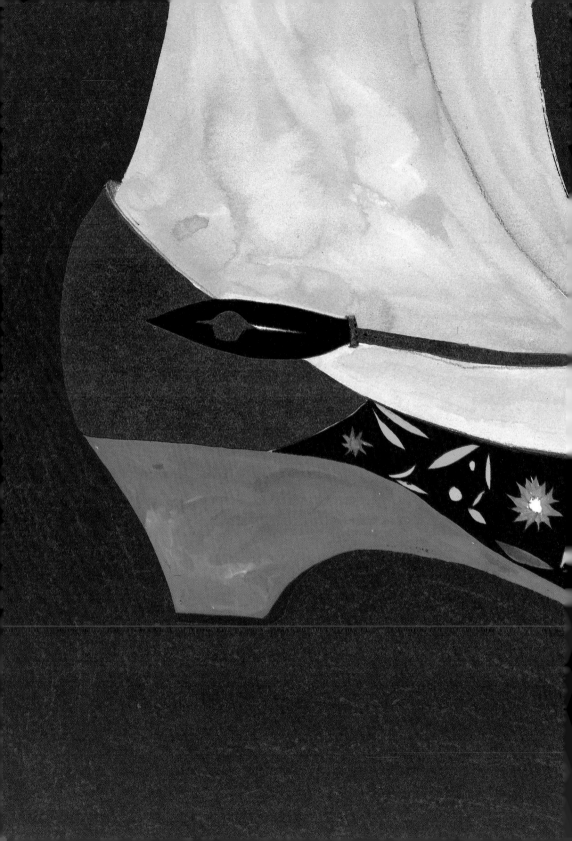

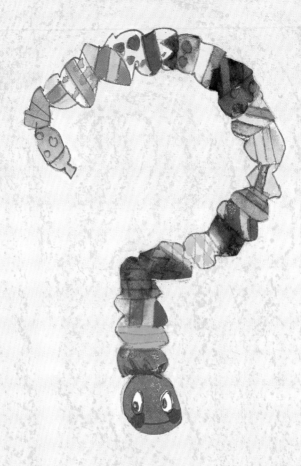

Oxford University Press, Walton Street, Oxford OX2 6DP

Oxford New York Toronto
Delhi Bombay Calcutta Madras Karachi
Petaling Jaya Singapore Hong Kong Tokyo
Nairobi Dar es Salaam Cape Town
Melbourne Auckland

and associated companies in
Beirut Berlin Ibadan Nicosia

Oxford is a trade mark of Oxford University Press

British Library Cataloguing in Publication Data
Wildsmith, Brian
Whose shoes?
I. Title
823'.914[J] PZ7
ISBN 0-19-272145-3

Printed in Hong Kong